DISLOCATIONS

First published by Charco Press 2022
Charco Press Ltd., Office 59, 44-46 Morningside Road, Edinburgh EH10 4BF

Copyright © Sylvia Molloy, 2010
First published in Spanish as *Desarticulaciones* by Eterna Cadencia (Argentina)
English translation copyright © Jennifer Croft, 2022

The rights of Sylvia Molloy to be identified as the author of this work and of
Jennifer Croft to be identified as the translator of this work have been asserted by
them in accordance with the Copyright, Designs and Patents Act 1988.

Work published with funding from the 'Sur' Translation Support Programme
of the Ministry of Foreign Affairs of Argentina / Obra editada en el marco
del Programa 'Sur' de Apoyo a las Traducciones del Ministerio de Relaciones
Exteriores de la República Argentina.

A CIP catalogue record for this book is available from the British Library.

ISBN: 9781913867355
e-book: 9781913867362

www.charcopress.com

Edited by Fionn Petch
Cover designed by Pablo Font
Typeset by Laura Jones
Proofread by Fiona Mackintosh

Sylvia Molloy

DISLOCATIONS

Translated by
Jennifer Croft

CHARCO PRESS

For M.L., no longer with us but still here

I need to write these texts while she's still with us, before death strikes or before she shuts down altogether; I need to try and understand this being but not being here on the part of a person who is coming apart before my very eyes. I need to do it this way in order to keep going, to hold onto a relationship that keeps going in spite of ruination – that subsists, although all that's (barely) left is words.

DISCONNECTION

We went to see her one afternoon and, while I was busy making sure all was in order, E. wound up talking with her in her bedroom, where she spends a good part of the day, looking out the window at the meagre sliver of sky left between two buildings. She told me something that I'm not sure she knew she was telling me, E. said when we went home, she told me that as a child she went with an aunt to visit an older relative who was in the hospital and gravely ill, connected to a machine, and that at some point when they were alone with this ailing relative her aunt had indicated with her head, nodding, kind of – she demonstrated it for me, E. says, reproducing it in turn, this indication – and M.L. had crouched down and unplugged the machine that had been breathing on behalf of the patient. And that after that, they'd left.

E. tells me she doesn't know what triggered this story, nor whether she realised she was telling it, but it was as though she needed to tell me, she says, or tell someone, maybe she's never told anyone before. Or maybe she made it up, I think, wondering whether machines kept anyone alive in the 1920s, unless perhaps it happened later, and she simply tells the story as though it happened when she was a child, to diminish her responsibility for killing someone. We'll never know, of course, since she's already forgotten the story. Not that it matters.

I read over what I've written, and something occurs to me, something obvious, perhaps: Was she asking for something, from us?

RHETORIC

As her memory goes, I realise she resorts to a politeness that is ever more refined, as though delicate manners might compensate for any absence of mind. It's curious to think that sentences so well-articulated – because she hasn't forgotten the structure of language: you might even say she thinks about it more now that night is falling inside her head – will not lodge in any recollection. When I got there this morning she was sleeping deeply, after yesterday's frenetic dispute. She opened her eyes, and I said hello, and she said, 'How nice to wake up and see friendly faces.' I don't believe she recognised us – individually, I mean. Two days ago, before her crisis, I asked how she was feeling, and she said, 'I'm good because you're here.' Today she told the nurse, 'You're looking very pretty, your face looks great today,' although it was the first time she had ever seen her, and although the nurse did not speak Spanish. I translated, and the nurse took an immediate liking to her. She had also been immediately liked, I remember, by a Black Dominican waitress who served us one day in a café, back when she was still roving the city without getting lost. The woman overheard us speaking Spanish, and when we told her where we were from, she couldn't believe it, she told us she would never have imagined we were Latin American due to our 'refinement'. Like lightning M.L. answered: 'Refinement is a quality all honourable people possess.'

To a friend who hasn't seen her in a long time, when I bring her for a visit: 'Would you like me to give you the tour?' And to our surprise, she guides us from room to room as though she'd just moved into her apartment, as though we were here for the first time.

LOGIC

She operates flawlessly by deduction, thus proving – yet again – that you do not have to have your wits about you to think in a rational way. As always, she asks after E., although at this point the name has hollowed out for her; whenever she sees her she still says, as we take our leave, give my regards to E., as though E. weren't standing there. Today I tell her E. is tired from a long day in court. Well of course, she answers, you two and that horrible trial. No, I'm quick to contradict her, no, as though to banish any real effects her words might have, no, God forbid: That's where she works, in court, E. is a lawyer. I sense this disappoints her. I believe her explanation, perfectly logical (court, therefore on trial), was more to her liking. It was certainly more exciting.

QUESTION SET

I recall another instance of her logic, this one poetic. One day, when I was still taking her to the clinic where they were taking stock of her gradual loss of memory, I asked her to tell me what kinds of questions asked. Today they asked me what a bird and a tree have in common. I was intrigued and said: So what did you answer? That they both know how to fly, she told me, so pleased with herself. I thought the question must have been something else, although I never managed to learn what. Or perhaps it wasn't. Perhaps they do have something in common, the tree and the bird.

Recalling this incident brings to mind another that doesn't quite involve her. On one of those visits to the clinic, while she was being examined, and I was waiting, I happened to be sharing the waiting room with another woman who had been stripped of her memory, accompanied by a young couple, perhaps her son and his wife. They were also waiting for her to be examined. I listened to the couple as they asked her questions, prepping her so she would get them right. Who is the president of the United States? What is the capital of this country? They wanted her to look good, not to do badly. They didn't ask her what a tree had in common with a bird.

TRANSLATION

Like rhetoric, the faculty for translation does not get lost, at least not until the very end. This I confirmed once more today as I spoke with L. I asked her if the doctor had been informed that M.L. had had a dizzy spell, and she told me he had. Out of curiosity, I asked her how she had conveyed this information, given that L. doesn't speak English. M.L. interpreted for me, she said. Which means that while M.L. is incapable of saying that she has had a dizzy spell, that is, incapable of remembering the state of being dizzy, she is capable all the same of translating into English L.'s message that she, M.L., has had a dizzy spell. It is a way of accessing a momentary identity, a momentary existence, by means of that efficiently transmitted (transmuted) speech. For a second, in that translation, M.L. is there.

IDENTIKIT

How does someone who remembers nothing speak in the first person? What is the location of that 'I', once the memory has come undone? I am told that the last time she was taken to the hospital, she was asked her name, and she said, 'Petra'. One of the people who was with her saw this response as a sign that she was still capable of irony; she was indignant at the dim-wittedness of the doctor who 'simply didn't get it'. I think: if there is irony, and not merely the desire to think her capable of irony, then it is one of those ironies people say is sad. Petra, petrified, turned to stone, to say who she is?

RUNNING ON EMPTY

Twice her memory has burst its banks, giving rise to unconnected snippets of a past that had seemed lost forever, like islands a tsunami leaves when it recedes. At these times, it is as though she's awakened from a long period of apathy, suffused with febrile thrill: she speaks without pause, asks questions, makes plans, seems efficient and clear-sighted. On one such occasion she started giving orders, Don't send that text to the printer's yet, I need to see if there are any errors in it, and then we have to give it to X., and I need to talk to that girl who's in charge of V.'s affairs. (She hadn't spoken of V. in years, but I dare not ask about her, I stick to her script.) Yes, I say, don't worry, I won't send anything before you've had a chance to review it.

I actually don't think it would be hard for her to correct the style of a text, even if she didn't understand any of what it said. I myself consult her now and then: Is this how you say such and such? She invariably gives the right answers.

SHE ENJOYS EXCELLENT HEALTH

In fact, I don't remember ever having seen her sick, or nothing more than just a cold, a virus: some minor indisposition, as people used to say. Then again maybe I can't remember her being sick because for years I needed her to be healthy, Freudianly *certissima*, sound, to counterbalance my own malaise and constant toing and froing. Now, when people talk about illnesses in front of her, more than once I have asked her about her health, feeling slightly hypocritical, curious to know how aware she is of her memory loss. She always responds in the same way, that she has never been sick, that is, that she has never had a serious illness, I am basically a very healthy person, in that sense I've been lucky.

NARRATIVE LIBERTY

There are no witnesses left to a certain part of my life, the part her memory has taken with it. That loss that might cause me anguish is curiously liberating: there is no one to correct me now if I decide to make things up. In her presence, I recount some personal anecdote to L., who knows little about M.L.'s past and nothing about mine, and to make the story better I invent certain details, several of them. L. laughs, and M.L., too, enjoys it, neither of them questioning the veracity of what I'm saying, even what never occurred. Then again, maybe I'm making up everything I'm writing now. Ultimately no one could say otherwise.

FAREWELL

She's asleep, you can go. I don't know if she's asleep, sometimes she just looks like that. No, no, she's sleeping, see how she's relaxed her lips, which she always keeps so tight, I promise you, you can go. Let me at least give her a kiss on the cheek. You'll wake her up, it isn't worth it, I'll tell her you were here, she'll forget immediately anyway. But it's not the same, I protest. No, it's not the same.

EROTIC FASCINATION

Not long ago, I was unable to resist the temptation of mentioning H., just to see how she would take it. Do you remember anything about him? I asked, noticing that the name, although recognisable to her, didn't seem to provoke any reaction. No, but if I saw him I'm sure I'd remember, she answered. I thought: She'll never see him because he died a while ago, and she can't recognise people from photographs. Who is that, she sometimes asks, pointing to a picture of her mother. I also thought: Yet this is the man who subjected her to such extraordinary sexual excesses, which he made me observe, fully clothed, seated in a chair in front of them. It's lucky she doesn't remember him with her, and that she doesn't remember it was I who watched them.

QUOTE EXERCISE

She remembers poems, fragments of Aristophanes in Greek, a few poems by Darío. Quotes arise unexpectedly, this or that sentence by Borges. Today (but what is 'today' to her?) she recalled snippets of verses of a starkly neoclassical character, something about seizing the Iberian lion by its mane, and for a second I thought they were from that part of the national anthem that no one sings, but no, they were even more bellicose, even triter. I asked her why she would remember those verses, and she answered – perfectly reasonably – that that it must have been because they had unusual words in them that appealed to her when she was a child, like the verb 'to seize'. What she is saying makes sense, I think, a lot of sense, even. How can she be the same person who asks me, for the thousandth time, just as soon as we've finished our tea, if it is cold outside, and if I'd like to have some tea?

But the quotes that stick are those that come from the doxa of the bourgeoisie, those that make some reference to good manners, to those codes.

BLINDNESS

For some time I entertained a theory that might just be correct. I remembered that it had always been hard for Borges to speak in public, to the point that when he was awarded the national prize for literature, he had to ask someone else to read his acceptance speech. I used to identify with that shyness: I could barely teach a class and had to imagine that nobody was watching me in order not to stutter. Until it occurred to me that Borges had only been able to overcome this obstacle (the voice that shrinks, not wanting to come out, and then when it finally does, it trembles) upon becoming blind, because then he could no longer see his audience, which was like thinking his audience was not there.

Now, when I visit her, the opposite happens. I talk and talk (she contributes nothing to the conversation) and I tell her funny stories, and I make things up, as I have already said, with ever-increasing facility. And I don't need to imagine myself blind because she's the one who cannot see, who does not recognise, does not remember. Talking with someone who's lost their memory is like talking to a blind person, describing to them whatever you can see: your interlocutor witnesses nothing, cannot contradict what you have said.

EXPECTATIONS

Yesterday was, for some reason, a particularly pathetic visit, that is, I wound up feeling pretty blue. Mine are the only feelings I can account for; hers are almost impossible to read at this point, beyond a smile or some exclamation of pain. I ended up blue; I don't think she ended up anything. She was expecting me when I arrived, meaning that she had been prepared to be expecting me, told periodically that I was about to arrive, in order to generate, albeit for a moment, an attitude of expectation. I wonder what would happen if my visits weren't announced, whether on seeing me arrive she would recognise me right away; I prefer not to find out. Yesterday when I got there she was in her chair, sitting very still and – as people used to say, in fact as she herself might have said in another era – all fixed up. The fact of seeing her dressed well and well-groomed, knowing that other hands had dressed her and groomed her, always adds to the pathos, increases that sense of non-personhood that I sometimes perceive in her, of a non-personhood that is – paradoxically – quite dignified. Her face lights up when she sees me, I've been expecting you, she says, like a character written by Rulfo.

BIRTHDAY

Her birthday is in two days. I bring her a gift ahead of time, a stereo, since hers has broken down, and music keeps her company now that books no longer can. I insert a tango CD I find lying there, instrumental tangos, but quietly she sings along, the little snippets of lyrics she has left, *yo adivino el parpadeo, volver con la frente marchita las nieves del tiempo, no habrá más penas ni olvidos, desde que se fue triste vivo yo*, as she studies minutely the message I wrote her on her birthday card, puzzled, disconcerted, wanting to get a grip on it.

RECOLLECTION

I keep finding myself saying, Remember such and such?
When obviously her response will be in the negative,
and I get frustrated with myself for having asked her the
question, not so much frustrated with her, since the fact
of not remembering is completely meaningless for her,
but with myself, with my insistence on these pleas for
confirmation, like raking water uphill. Why don't I just
say, 'You know, one time…' and tell her the story of the
memory as though it were a new one, as though it were
someone else's anecdote that makes no demands on her?
I have done it that way, I've told her how once we went
to Buenos Aires together and they stopped us at customs
because she was carrying a little baggie of white dust,
and the officials didn't believe her when she told them it
was laundry detergent, You think we don't have laundry
detergent here, señora, and they kept us waiting for hours
while they analysed it. She laughs, she thinks I'm exagge-
rating, I did that? she says, in retrospective wonderment.
Oh you did, I assure her, and this other time you got
your plane ticket for free by transporting a mink stole
from a New York furrier to an Argentine client. And that
time they didn't stop you, I have no idea how, it was the

31

middle of summer, and you went right in with that fur on. She continues smiling, somewhere between pleased and confused.

I guess I can't get used to not saying 'remember' because I'm still trying to maintain, in those slivers of our shared past, the furtive ties that bind us together. And because in order to keep up a conversation – to keep up a relationship – we have to recollect things together, or pretend to, even when she – that is, her memory – has already left my memory behind.

LISTS

There was a time before these visits when, realising – if indeed a person can completely realise – that she was starting to lose her memory, she'd make lists of the things she needed to do, or the things she had to make sure not to forget. I remember seeing a couple of those lists, tacked up to a chalkboard in the kitchen, and another among some papers I ended up organising at some point, scrawled in an uncertain hand, almost illegible, not to say unintelligible, lists where people and objects coexisted seemingly at random. They reminded me of the ones my mother used to dictate to me so as not to forget, Write this down: Enrique, begonias, dining table, minced meat. They were lists that only she could understand, though that is the case with almost any list: in the absence of its author, there is no one who can give it meaning.

They were, above all, lists that M.L. forgot or neglected to check. I know this from my own experience. Today, before going to visit her, I went by the pharmacy to pick up a couple of things I'd been wanting to take her. Only when I got to her place did I realise I'd forgotten something – in other words, only then did I take a look at my list.

ON PROPER LANGUAGE

'Does she still recognise you?' people ask me. 'How do you know she still recognises you?' I guess I don't really know, but I tend to say that yes, of course, she knows who I am, just to deflect any further solicitude. Yet at this point I suspect that if L. didn't tell her my name, before handing her the phone when I call her, or before opening the door for me when I come over, I might be a stranger to her. Even my name has lost its former capacity to summon, no longer providing her much information. It does cause her to ask me about E. and 'the cat', but it is clear to me that she does not know who E. is: she asks me about her in her presence, How is your companion doing? As far as the mention of 'the cat', like that, anonymously, it's yet another proof of her good manners. Or perhaps a distant memory of some platonic archetype, as if she were asking after all felinity.

Yesterday I discovered that I had become even less myself for her sake. I called her, and although L. handed her the phone saying who was calling, she still used the most generic form of address – 'tú', and not the Rioplatense 'vos' – throughout our conversation. It was a cordial, perfectly proper conversation in a Spanish we had never spoken to each other before. When it was over, I sensed I'd lost yet more of what had been left of me.

RE-PRODUCTION

As I write about her, I'm tempted to describe her as she was before, specifically when I first met her, to put her back together at the moment of her greatest strength, instead of in the midst of her implosion. But that isn't the point, I remind myself, that is not the point: I'm not writing to patch up holes and make people (or myself) think that there's nothing to see here, but rather to bear witness to unintelligibilities and breaches and silences. That is my continuity, that of the scribe. But I'm comforted when she occasionally emerges from her detachment – itself perhaps a form of wisdom – with some impertinent remark that takes me back to how she used to be: witty, ironic, snobby, critical, at times even malicious. Can she have been all those things, or am I remembering wrong?

DISAPPOINTMENT

Over the phone, she tells me something I've never heard her say before, something that breaks with the serenity I've been attributing to her, something that, for a moment, might indicate an awareness of which I haven't thought her capable. We're talking about L., I say she's lucky to have her there to take care of her, and she says yes, that she is very lucky, but that she feels bad giving her so much trouble. Oh, you don't give anyone any trouble, I tell her, to reassure her, and because I realise that this isn't just a set phrase she's employing, yet another proof of her good manners. I think I do, she answers in a dejected tone. Sounds like you're a little down, I say, and she says, Yes, very down, in the same faint, dull voice. She realises, I think. She knows. This isn't just politeness.

SOUNDING OUT

She's been making up words for some time now, as if talking to herself in an impenetrable language. Yesterday when I went to see her she kept saying, Hukuhuku. I asked her what it meant; Nothing, she said, It's a word I made up. Then she started counting the syllables on her fingers, rhythmically, Hu-ku-hu-ku. That's too bad, she said, staring at her pinky: One syllable too few. Why don't you add another one, I suggested; it could be Hu-ku-hu-ku-hu. She tried again, and this time there was a finger for each syllable. Whew, she said, smiling.

HANDWRITING

She isn't able to sign her name, not because she doesn't remember what her name is (I think), but because she can no longer write. The first time I noticed it she had started on her signature but stalled halfway through, like someone who's forgotten the rest of a poem they thought they knew by heart. Since then I've tried to get her to sign things on multiple occasions, on whatever pretext, just to see if she is able to get the momentum to complete her name, but it has always been for naught. Gone are the letters, the written name that is another form of being in the world.

Sometimes, putting my papers in order, I come across something she wrote, an index card or a page that might have gone into some article we did together. They're notes that have outlived their usefulness, but I can't bring myself to toss them out. They make up a little heap in one desk drawer, snippets of writing that reassure me that at some point, she was here.

ON THE NECESSITY OF A WITNESS

Today in the hour I spent in her house I spoke at length with R., the woman who takes care of her when L. isn't there. I asked her if the capital of her country was as dangerous as people said it was, and she said, No, it's really not any worse than any other Latin American city. M.L. nodded with a smile as though following the conversation, All cities are dangerous, she said. But mine used to be more so, R. said, in the guerrilla era, and I know what I'm talking about. She went on to explain that she'd been on the police force in her country before coming to the U.S., an investigator, I believe she said, and that she had been the secretary of a colonel and of a general, as well, and that of course some innocents had perished, but lots of guerrillas had, too, and it became clear which regime we were discussing, and M.L. smiled as though hearing someone say that it was hot or cold out, or that it was raining, and I couldn't help but wonder how she might have reacted had she had any idea what R. was saying with such perfect serenity, this thing that reduced me to silence, this shocking and terrible thing that we could not comment on or share.

LIKE A BLIND MAN WITH
SEARCHING HANDS

When she started losing her memory (but that's not right: I can only really say 'when I noticed she was starting to lose her memory') she began to use her hands a lot. She'd get to a familiar place and start touching whatever was on the table, or a shelf, like a child, the kind of child you have to ready the house for, hiding certain things or placing them out of reach. She would pick something up and then set it back down but not quite in the place where she had found it, just slightly to the right, or to the left, like someone wanting to correct a mistake through rearrangement. All this in silence and absolute concentration. I never asked her why she was doing it, even though I did say a few times, again, as to a child, in irritation, 'Please don't touch anything.' It was hard for me to acknowledge that she had begun to rely, instinctively, on tactile memory. Like Greta Garbo from *Queen Christina*, she was remembering objects not to store them in her mind, but to orient herself in the present.

SECRET NAMES

People who love each other come up with new names, absurd appellations based on some secret or some shared experience nobody knows about, names that are sometimes childish, often foolish and obscene: it's the language of love, untranslatable. In a dream, I am speaking with A. over the phone, and suddenly E. comes by, and I say something to her using the name I used to use for A. On hearing me say that name, A., predictably, hangs up. It's just a dream.

Sometimes I think when I visit her that she had a name for me, also secret, that she definitely stopped using when I ended our relationship. Sometimes I think that somewhere in her Swiss-cheese memory that name must still be there, and in the same way we say Pablo when we mean to say Pedro, someday it's going to just slip out. It's never happened, and it won't happen: holding her tongue out of spite may be the last to go, hand in hand with her propriety.

COLLABORATION

Recently I had to talk in class about a novel I hadn't read in a long time, a novel we liked, she and I, and wrote a couple of articles about, together. That was at a time when both of us were having trouble writing, so we decided to do it together, to see if the collaboration helped us along enough that we could then keep going on our own. I don't know if we would have done it with another text, but this one, in particular, served as a challenge. I know the exercise worked for me, and afterwards my work came much more easily. I don't remember if that was the case for her.

When I reread the novel last week I was surprised by the clarity with which I remembered our conversations from back then; what I had said about this or that scene, what she had said, as though I could no longer read the book except according to that old reading we'd done together. As I discussed the novel in class, making our observations from back then as though they were brand new, I felt as though I were plagiarising us. Or rather: I felt like I was plagiarising her – she who does not recall having written those articles, who does not recall having read that novel, who cannot recollect Pedro Páramo, 'my mother's husband', 'living bile'.

51

CAT

The cat isn't well. The cat she rescued one Fourth of July, on the steps of an abandoned building, huddled terrified of the fireworks, the cat she never managed to domesticate: she isn't doing well. I think by the time she rescued her, she'd already forgotten how to interact with cats, you forget those rituals of seduction, too, when you lose your memory. I recall that the cat hid under a piece of furniture for weeks, and she made her come out by jabbing her with a broomstick, like a wilful little child.

In the end, the cat gets worse, won't eat, keeps crying, and we have to get rid of her. Someone takes care of it; not I. For weeks, the cat's dishes and water bowl and litter box remain in their place. M.L. doesn't notice she's gone, She must be in the bedroom, she says. In the end, she seems to forget, if that verb makes sense. Just in case, I never bring up cats when I visit.

CORPOREAL TASTES

For years, she refused to eat certain things, I think as much out of personal preference as bourgeois prejudice. Garlic and onion were out of the question, part of a group she dismissed out of hand as greasy diner fare. Certain meals fell into the same category, mostly heavy stews, which a certain friend and I would often order on purpose, every time we went out to eat with her, often with disastrous effects on our stomachs, which made her happy, since she felt it proved her right.

For years, she didn't eat meat, either, though that wasn't snobbery so much as conviction.

Now, as they say about obstinate children whose tastes soon change, she eats everything, which is to say, a little bit of everything is served to her. She doesn't know what she's eating: I've seen her put a piece of meat or a spoonful of onion soup in her mouth, and it's made me feel an agonising pity. Sometimes she doesn't even know what eating is: I'm told she forgets when she has to chew and when she doesn't, that sometimes she swallows whole pieces of food and others chews on yogurt.

I remember other amnesias of the body, as with N.'s mother, who, in addition to having forgotten how to eat would ask what legs were for: She'd laugh when she was told that they were used for walking. I remember my own mother, who, I suspect, choked to death (though no one was ever willing to confirm this) because she'd forgotten what it was to swallow.

GOOD-LOOKING

You're looking very pretty, she tells me, as she usually does when, on arrival, I lean down to kiss her cheek. You, too, I tell her, as usual, too, as though we are rehearsing, for the thousandth time, some comedy of manners. But today I deviate from the script, add: 'You're very good-looking today,' and I feel as though I've put quotation marks around 'good-looking', such an old-fashioned term. Suddenly I remember a song my sister and I overheard our aunt singing to herself one day, a song that later we sang over and over: 'I'm not good-looking, I'm not good-looking, and I don't want to be, and I don't want to be, because good-looking girls, because good-looking girls, go bad as bad can be, go bad as bad can be.' And I say to M.L., Do you remember, I bet you sang it when you were younger, too, and her face brightens into a smile, and she sings with me. And then, unexpectedly, ten minutes later she sings the whole thing, all over again. Then she sings it again. Then sings it again. Then again.

FINANCES

Once a year her accountant comes to see her to figure out her taxes; the procedure is always the same. He is ushered in, and she greets him as though she knows who he is; he sits down at the table with me, and I start handing him the necessary papers, while from the couch she asks what's going on. She gets agitated when she hears the word 'taxes', says it makes her nervous, Do I need to pay this man, she asks, Where did I put my money, or – sometimes – Do I have any money to pay him?

On one occasion the accountant called to say that he was running late, and before L. could pick up, M.L. did, speaking English, hanging up immediately, and when L. asked her what he'd said, she was forced to admit she had absolutely no idea. So there we were, waiting, while she kept asking every few minutes what we were doing. When we told her we were waiting for the accountant, she said, dryly, 'He could have called to let us know he was running late, it's a bit inconsiderate, wouldn't you say?' When we told her he had called, and that she was the one who had answered, she asked, 'What was it he said?'

He had said he'd be an hour late. We learned that when, an hour later, the doorbell rang.

BOTTLED UP

A. asks after her, it's been years since she saw her, she thinks of her often, she says, about a trip to Spain they took together, both of them invited to the same symposium. It was nice to travel with her, to be in cahoots, we laughed a lot, she told me things about her past, she said it wasn't good to go around keeping it all bottled up, that's how she put it, I still can't believe what happened with her father, wasn't it awful? Yeah, I say, her father passed away before she was even born: this is a story I know well. That's what they told her, A. tells me, but she told me how awful it was to learn years later that he hadn't actually died, he'd simply abandoned her and her mother and gone to live with someone else.

I feel like something is collapsing, to the point that I change the subject. How could I not know the story of her father, when she's recounted it multiple times over the course of the forty-five years that I've known her? How is it possible that what she's told me about her childhood – that after the death of her father, from tuberculosis, I think, her mother had to go and work because he'd left them with nothing, that she was practically raised by her grandmother, her mother's mother, who lived with them, and that they formed a kind of feminine trio that was as noble as it was pathetic – is all a lie, the death of her father a necessary fabrication to cover up the ignominy, the abandonment? But above all: how am I supposed to accept that she told me the ersatz version, that only now does her illness permit her to breach such interdictions, and then only in the presence of a third party with whom she has almost no contact?

The next time I see her I ask her in passing if she remembers her father, and she says no because she was very little, but that she does remember one day when she was told she wouldn't be going to school because her papa had died, That's what they told me, she says as if she's no longer used to this kind of terminology, 'your papa', and I said, How is that the school's fault, That's what I told them, she tells me, enchanted by her mischievousness in childhood. And as with my conversation with A., I change the subject.

So then I think that what if what she told A. is true. But then again maybe it isn't, maybe A. has mixed up that story with another one she was told by someone else, or perhaps M.L. is making up the news of his death that she thinks she remembers, even though I know it's unlikely, the oddness of that 'your papa' is too precise. I'm tempted to ask her about her father again, but I know that I won't, and I know that deep down, it doesn't matter. What is difficult for me to accept is that there was something she had bottled up so tightly she had to keep it quiet even with me. What is difficult for me to accept is that there may be other things bottled up like this that I will never be allowed to know.

SER AND ESTAR

The most difficult thing about Spanish, for learners, is the difference between *ser* and *estar*. I remember all the times, years ago, I had to correct, in vain, my students saying *soy cansado* and *estoy una chica buena*. Closer to home, at home, I take note of E.'s efforts to master the distinction. Yesterday I overheard her on the phone with a mutual friend, talking about me, and boasting her tenuous knowledge, she remarked, 'Ella es ausente.' I laughed, and for the thousandth time I explained to E. why you can't say it like that: 'es' means permanently, 'she is absent', as a condition of her being. Not a temporary state, like 'está'. But then I think, but actually you could say it like that, if you were speaking of M.L. She *is* absent, eternally so.

And yet, and yet. Today, I called her as I do every evening, to ask about her day, and like every night, she answered, 'Nothing to report.' But today there was something to report: when L. handed her the phone, saying, 'It's S.', she answered by saying, 'How's it going, Molloy?' Even now, in some recess of her mind, I'm not totally, permanently absent. I can be temporarily there.

MEMORY'S PASSAGEWAYS

Starting a few years ago – I can't say since when exactly, perhaps since the attack on the Twin Towers that disrupted my sense of time and space – I have been visited, with some regularity, by distant memories. That's not quite right: they don't visit me so much as burst in unexpectedly and derail my already fragile train of thought. What must be for some, I suppose, a source of nostalgic pleasure or bittersweet melancholy becomes, for me, a burden that is often too much to bear. I want to be the proprietor of my memory, not for my memory to be in charge of me. This lurking of the past, almost constant, not only interrupts my present, but also literally invades it. I wake up and decide to get up, think of having coffee, and I picture the kitchen in my parents' house, not my own kitchen, where my coffeemaker is in fact awaiting me. In no way does my house resemble that one, and yet, whenever I picture a part of it – when, for instance, I think of something on the first floor while doing something on the second – I picture its equivalent in that other house, as though the staircase I'll be going down were capable of taking me back, with no gaps or sutures, to that other time and place. When I'm downstairs in my home, whatever noise I hear from upstairs, the scraping of a chair when someone stands up, instantly conjures the sewing room where my mother and my aunt hem while listening to radio plays. In the beginning, this persistent and disordered contamination attracted me as a possible source of stories. Now it makes me uncomfortable: more than that, it genuinely disturbs me.

I wonder if M.L.'s memory loss has something to do with the arbitrary exacerbation of my own. If somehow I'm compensating, proving to myself that my memory recollects, recollects even when I don't want it to. I wonder, too, if the same might not have happened to M.L., if she might also have suffered from this excess of memory, this contamination of the present with the past, before she started losing it.

FRACTURE

A week ago, I got hit by a bicycle, breaking my leg. I spent a few days in the hospital, made groggy by painkillers, in a cloud in which – I am told – I spoke animatedly with anyone who came to visit me and abundantly over the phone. I remember none of this: not the people I called, nor what I said to my visitors. I did remember, on the other hand, on one of those interminable days as I stared at the wall where a bulky TV set was hanging, that M.L. had broken her femur some years ago, and that her stay in the hospital had unhinged her more than usual. She heard the woman in the next bed talking to somebody, and she said, 'Who let those people in, somebody needs to ask them to leave.' On noticing a television similar to the one I myself was watching from my hospital bed, she said to us in great irritation: 'What is that suitcase doing there, that's not the place for it, it needs to be taken down.' She thought she was in her house and tried to put things back in order, restore tranquillity. What she refused to believe was that the leg that had been operated on and bandaged up was hers. She looked at it and kept asking whose it was; when we told her it was hers, she'd say, surprised, Oh really? As though coming to some sudden revelation.

In the week that has passed since my accident, during which time I haven't been able to move much, or read much because I can't get myself to concentrate, my memory has started working at a fevered pace. I've recollected in minute detail my mother's family, my father's family, I've thought about my sister, I've relived the years we spent in Paris, I've gone over other long periods in Paris with other people, they've come to me day and night, without letting me sleep, without releasing me, pieces of the past, from the trivial to the traumatic, with an annoying insistence, as if total repose and the inability to think in a sustained way had given rise to a bottomless pit that had to be filled so that I would not surrender to panic. And I think of M.L. – who during her convalescence did not experience that hypersaturation worthy of Funes – M.L. who didn't even remember having broken her leg, even when said leg was right in front of her. I think that perhaps in that instance – and only that one – she had the better deal.

WHO CAN'T READ OR WRITE

After a trip to Buenos Aires I went to visit her, taking her some of the more famous alfajores, I brought you a little present from the motherland, I said, holding out the box. Oh my, how nice, she answered, reaching for it like an overeager child. Look at the box, I said, and I realised she was already looking at it, and I also realised that she could no longer read. Alfajores, I told her, thinking that soon the time would come when she would no longer know the meaning of the word 'alfajor'.

WHO CAN READ AND WRITE: PERHAPS

After another trip to Buenos Aires, I go to visit her, taking her alfajores again. I put the box on the table, This is for you, I say. She looks at the box, reads 'Havanna' and asks me what it is. I point to the drawing of the alfajor on the box, and she understands, Yum, alfajores, she says, like a mollified child. Ten minutes later, pointing to the box, she asks me what it is. She can't read 'Havanna' now but, looking at the word that comes before the brand name, she says, triumphant, 'Alfonsina'. In vain I point to the drawing of the alfajor; I don't know what that is, she says.

ALFAJORES III

Another trip, more alfajores. I brought you a little gift from Buenos Aires, I tell her yet again. She opens the package, looks at the box, reads out loud: 'Havanna', Yum, alfajores, she says.

PROJECTION

I'm talking about an exacerbation of my memory, about the contamination of my recollections, about the lists I make so that I don't forget, and of course about slips, too, oversights. My own oversights, not hers: to be able to say that a person has forgotten, they have to have, at least, some basic ability to recall, a word that, for her, no longer has meaning. (Even though today she 'remembered' the nickname she'd been given as a girl and that only her family had ever called her: she kept saying it, amazed, as though it belonged to someone else.)

During my time in the hospital, after my accident, I had a strange dream. I dreamed I was with a famous grande dame of Manhattan who had died a few years earlier. Alive in my dream, she was lamenting not having gone to the first Yves Saint Laurent fashion show, since afterwards she'd been such an enthusiastic patron of his work over the course of his career, and he had referred to her as 'la plus chic du monde', and in my dream, I was trying to console her, I was saying that I had the whole catwalk in my head, and I could show it to her, because in essence my mind was a film projector that contained all things. Just like that, on one of the walls of her library,

I started projecting the fashion show, down to the littlest details, with my head, which was now the Aleph.

I think: How much, in another era, M.L. would have delighted in this cross between the literary and the frivolous, how well she would have understood that dream. I think: I dare not ask her if she remembers Borges, even less Saint Laurent, lest she reply that if she saw them she's sure she'd remember.

WISECRACKS

The visits are less and less amusing, she's no longer as together, I say to a friend, she seems more and more out of it. As if now she were losing, too, her quickness on her feet, her ability to jump in with an untimely recollection or some witty non sequitur. She repeats her own bons mots, the old 'I'm good because you're here.' 'Don't you reuse yours?' my friend asks, quite rightly.

There is another explanation, of course. That the ghastly originality of the illness is becoming, for me, a cliché, another mode, predictable now, of communication. I have eased into illness, as well, into its rhetoric; nothing surprises me anymore. This ought to be a consolation, probably, but for some reason I find it alarming. Because I'll no longer have anything to write about?

PREMONITION

I had a strange episode that I'm recording here because it's the only place where I really talk about memory these days, about M.L.'s memory that keeps leaving pieces by the roadside, but also – today, in any case – about mine. For several nights I'd slept poorly, had dreams about which I remembered next to nothing (they had to do with movement, with automobiles that couldn't brake – even with the parking brake on they kept sliding, inexorably, down ravines), dreams that left me in a bad place, extremely uneasy, trying to remember, to reconstruct, to grasp hold of fragments. But that day it was as if the dream, whatever it was, went on into my waking hours, as though my mind, independently of me, were going from the one to the other trying to capture some concrete unease, an anguish over something ominous that was about to occur but that had already occurred, something I couldn't formulate in my mind, much less put into words. I felt dizzy, I had to sit down, it was as if I suddenly had a hole in my brain through which something was overflowing, something that had happened at some remote time, but not in a dream, something I couldn't remember. Smile, said E., close your right eye, raise your left hand, and I realised she was making sure I wasn't having a stroke, It's fine, I said, in English, 'It's not a tumour', like Schwarzenegger in *Kindergarten Cop*; I said it without any certainty, just making the joke. Because there must have been something going on.

VOICE

She sounds different. She speaks in a hoarse voice now, as though she always had a cold. Or rather: like someone who has just woken up and is talking for the first time since falling asleep, with a certain difficulty, her voice still elsewhere, unaccustomed to being awake or to conversation. The voice of one who needs to clear her throat before making some apposite, even witty, remark. Her voice like mine when, many years ago, she would call me almost every morning, and on hearing me, she'd say, 'It's obvious you haven't talked to anybody yet.' Except that in her voice nothing ever gets clarified; everything remains in a fog: it is indeed as though she hadn't spoken to anyone.

MOTHER TONGUE AND
MOTHERLAND

With no one, I increasingly realise, do I speak the language I speak with her, an at-home Spanish, if you will, except that it's from a home that was never altogether mine. A home from another era, inhabited by words that are no longer in favour, that perhaps were (or perhaps were not) favoured by our mothers or our grandmothers, words like *porrazo*, *mangangá*, *creída*, *chúcara*, and expressions used by friends in common who are now dead, *You don't say*, *It's like she was raised in a barn*. A Spanish pieced together from citations, but of course, what language isn't; to talk is to seek complicity: we understand each other, we know where we're from. Language, after all, creates roots and houses stories. When I talk to others – compatriots, let's say – sometimes I use one or another of these words or expressions, cautiously, seeking recognition. Sometimes it appears; sometimes it does not.

When talking to her I feel – or I felt – connected to a past that is not entirely illusory. And with a place: that of *before*. Now I find myself speaking in a void: there is no longer a home, no longer a before. Only an echo chamber.

'IS THIS MOMENT COMING
OR GOING?'

I never tell her that I'll be traveling, so as not to upset her – only on my return do I tell her that I've been gone. During the trip itself I call her almost every night without telling her where I am, knowing it doesn't matter, that only the moment of hearing my voice is what is (perhaps) important, not where I'm calling from or when I'm returning. Still, I feel a little like a fraud, like when I call someone from my cell phone, at home, to say I can't go somewhere because I'm elsewhere.

Today I called her on my return and, knowing that only the announcement of departures upsets her, I told her that I had been traveling and that I had just returned. How long are you staying? she asked me. And with this she disarmed me completely, making me feel transient, out of place. No, no, I live here, I wanted to tell her. But it wasn't worth making the correction. Where is here for her (or for me)?

VOLVER

Last night I dreamed that she was as she was before, lucid, her memory intact. She was telling me that she had decided to return to Argentina, to go back to end her life there. She said it serenely, like someone who has made a decision after giving it a lot of thought; she was almost happy, even. She was smiling, shaking her head and tossing her hair, which was long, as she had never worn it, but in spite of this, I knew that it was her. On waking I remembered that in the afternoon I had been reading a homecoming tale in which a character returns to the country they left many years earlier with a desire to resume – or create – the life they think they remember and miss, a better life. Instead, they are met with a militarised country, arbitrary arrest, and, in the end, death. And I thought that somehow in my dream I was transferring that story to her, as though to improve that ruthless narrative. Because only total oblivion allows for unscathed return; in some sense, she's gone back already.

INTERRUPTION

I feel that leaving this story is leaving her, that by not recording our interactions anymore, I'm denying her something, a continuity to which only I, with my visits, can attest. I feel like I'm abandoning her. But in some sense she's the one who's been abandoning herself, so I won't feel guilty. Or just a little bit.

CHARCO PRESS

Director & Editor: Carolina Orloff
Director: Samuel McDowell

www.charcopress.com

Dislocations was published on
90gsm Munken Premium Cream paper.

The text was designed using Bembo 11.5 and ITC Galliard.

Printed in July 2022 by TJ Books
Padstow, Cornwall, PL28 8RW using responsibly
sourced paper and environmentally-friendly adhesive.